Bumblebee at Apple Tree Lane

SMITHSONIAN'S BACKYARD

For my parents, Chuck and Barbara, with all my love — L.G.

To Mom and Dan with much love and admiration — K^2

Published by Soundprints Division of Trudy Corporation, Norwalk, Connecticut.

Art Director: Diane Hinze Kanzler
Editor: Judy Gitenstein

First Edition 2000
10 9 8 7 6 5 4 3 2
Printed in Singapore

Acknowledgments:
   Our very special thanks to Dr. Beth B. Norden of the Department of Entomology at the Smithsonian Institution's National Museum of Natural History for her curatorial review.

Library of Congress Cataloging-in-Publication Data

Galvin, Laura Gates.
     Bumblebee at Apple Tree Lane / written by Laura Gates Galvin; illustrated by Kristin Kest. — 1st ed.
          p.   cm. — (Smithsonian's backyard)
     Summary: Bumblebee emerges from hibernation, builds a nest, lays eggs, and begins the process of creating a busy bumblebee colony.
     ISBN 1-56899-820-1
     1. Bumblebees—Juvenile fiction. [Bumblebees—Fiction.]   I. Kest, Kristin, ill.   II. Title.   III. Series.
PZ10.3.G153Bu   2000   99-043774
[E]—dc21   CIP
                                                                                    AC

Bumblebee at Apple Tree Lane

by Laura Gates Galvin

Illustrated by Kristin Kest

Soundprints

Where Children Discover...

In April, when the air is pleasantly cool and the sun shines brightly, southern New England is waking up after a long winter's nap. Dandelions dot green lawns, early-migrating birds have returned home from the south, and tiny new leaves adorn the branches of trees.

Behind a small stone-and-wood cottage on Apple Tree Lane, a fuzzy black-and-yellow bumblebee has just crawled out from underground after a long hibernation.

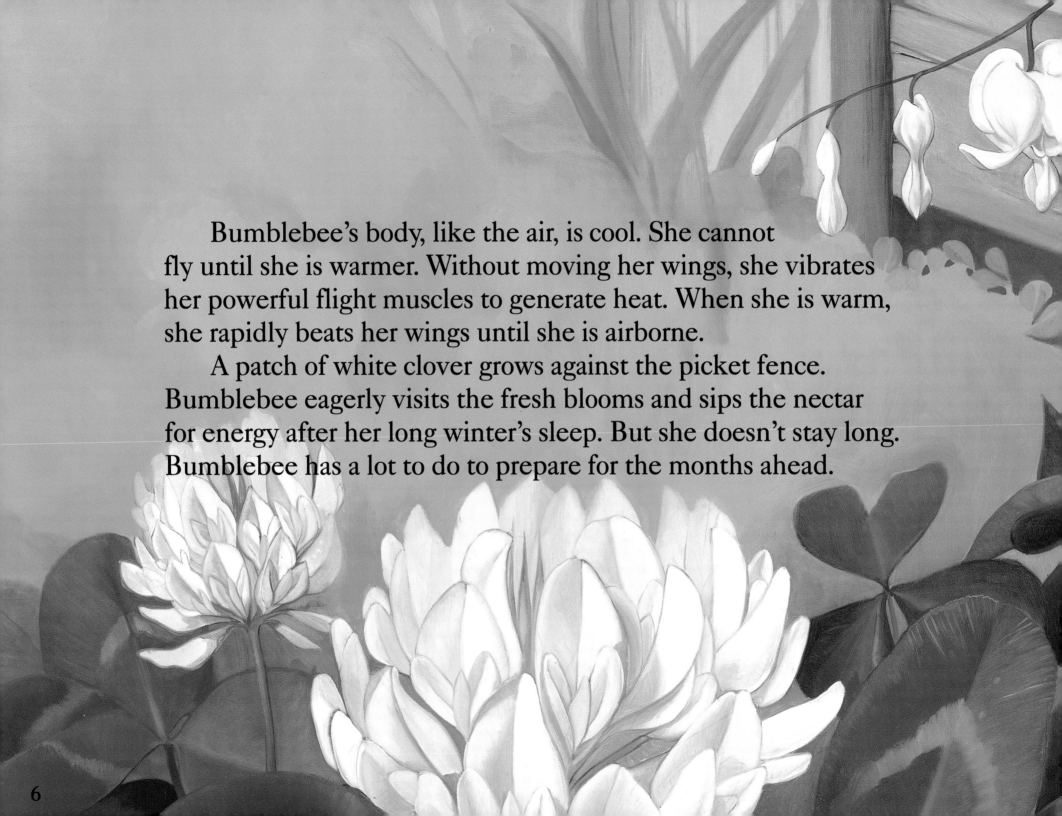

Bumblebee's body, like the air, is cool. She cannot fly until she is warmer. Without moving her wings, she vibrates her powerful flight muscles to generate heat. When she is warm, she rapidly beats her wings until she is airborne.

A patch of white clover grows against the picket fence. Bumblebee eagerly visits the fresh blooms and sips the nectar for energy after her long winter's sleep. But she doesn't stay long. Bumblebee has a lot to do to prepare for the months ahead.

Her first task is to find a homesite. She devotes the next few days to looking for an abandoned nest. A bird's nest or a mouse's nest would be just right for her. Bumblebee flies slowly, close to the ground, stopping often to investigate likely spots. Near the garage, in the hollow of a birch tree, she finds an abandoned field mouse's nest. She spends the next few days cleaning her new home.

After Bumblebee has removed all the leftover sticks and dirt from her nest, she begins to shape a little honey pot from wax which is pressed out from between her abdominal segments. When she is finished shaping the honey pot, she leaves her nest to visit more spring blossoms.

On this visit to the flowers, Bumblebee sips the nectar
and stores it in her crop, or stomach. When she returns
to her nest, Bumblebee fills the honey pot with the nectar.
She will save this nectar to drink on a rainy day.

Bumblebee builds another waxen cell, this one to be
used for her eggs. She lays eight eggs and covers them
with a wax cap. Like a brooding hen, Bumblebee settles
down on her nest and keeps her eggs warm.

Five days later, Bumblebee's eggs hatch into larvae. Bumblebee will continue to keep the larvae warm with her body, but she must also feed them. She flies directly to the apple tree near the back porch. As she crawls from one apple blossom to another, collecting nectar, pollen from the blossoms sticks to the thousands of tiny hairs that cover her body. Using her two fore legs and two mid legs, she brushes the pollen into the small baskets on her hind legs. When her pollen baskets are full, she returns to the nest. Bumblebee places the pollen in small pockets on the side of the honey pot for the larvae to eat.

A week later, Bumblebee's fat, well-fed larvae spin themselves into separate cocoons. Even though Bumblebee must still keep her cocoons warm, she is busy with other things, too. She makes more cells beside the clump of cocoons and lays more eggs in each cell. She also takes occasional trips outdoors for nectar.

Two weeks have passed. It is the middle of May and spring is in full bloom. The air is warmer, the days are longer, and the flowers are plentiful. Bumblebee has just helped her first set of bees out of their silken cocoons.

Eight damp, silvery-gray worker bees, all female, crawl to the honey pot for their first meal as adults.

Bumblebee's daughters are good workers. They will feed the next batches of larvae and help keep the nest clean. From glands in her body, Bumblebee releases a certain chemical scent that tranquilizes her daughters, causing them to take good care of her eggs and larvae. Until late summer, most of the eggs will hatch into females. And Bumblebee, the queen, will stay busy laying more and more eggs.

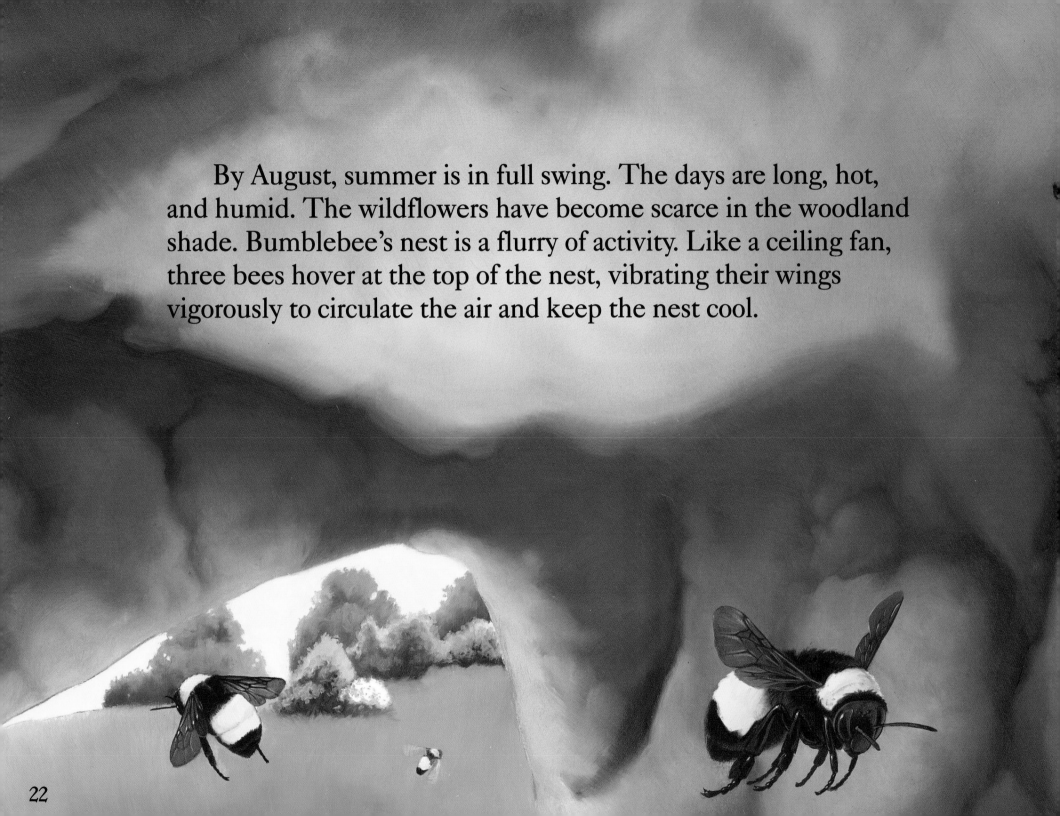

By August, summer is in full swing. The days are long, hot, and humid. The wildflowers have become scarce in the woodland shade. Bumblebee's nest is a flurry of activity. Like a ceiling fan, three bees hover at the top of the nest, vibrating their wings vigorously to circulate the air and keep the nest cool.

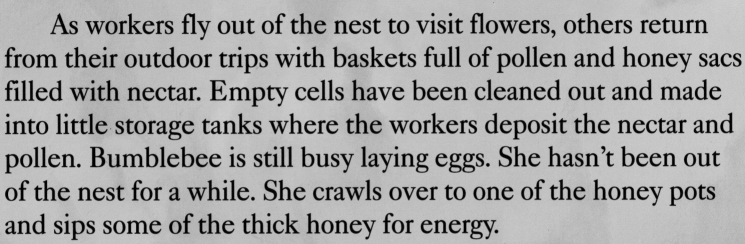

As workers fly out of the nest to visit flowers, others return from their outdoor trips with baskets full of pollen and honey sacs filled with nectar. Empty cells have been cleaned out and made into little storage tanks where the workers deposit the nectar and pollen. Bumblebee is still busy laying eggs. She hasn't been out of the nest for a while. She crawls over to one of the honey pots and sips some of the thick honey for energy.

While the bees work frantically, a carpenter ant enters the nest. An alarmed worker lifts her middle legs into the air to threaten the intruder. The ant doesn't move forward, but it doesn't leave the nest either. Without hesitating, the bee flips onto her back and opens her jaws, as if ready to bite. She also points her stinger in warning at the ant. This time the ant wastes no time and scurries out of the nest.

When October arrives, the air is brisk and the landscape is a burst of red, orange, and yellow. Bumblebee's last batches of eggs have hatched. But these eggs have not produced workers. Instead, they have developed into new queens, and males. These males won't stay in the nest long, but will leave to mate with young queens from other nests.

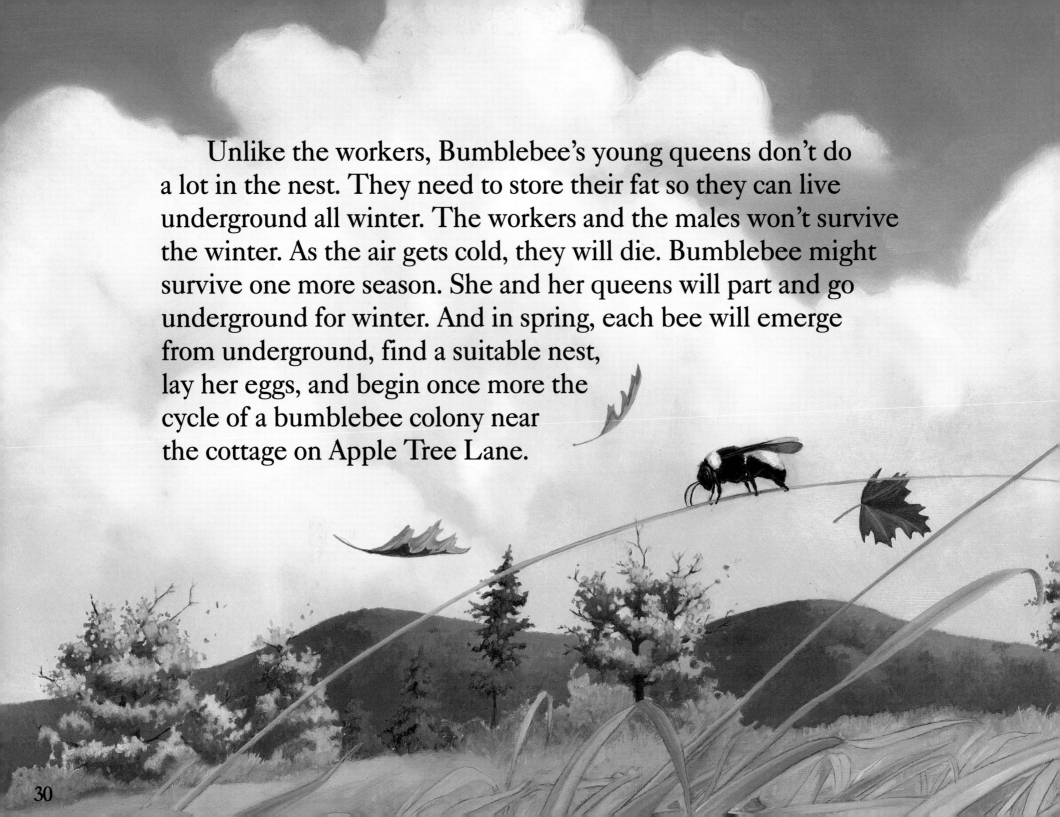

Unlike the workers, Bumblebee's young queens don't do a lot in the nest. They need to store their fat so they can live underground all winter. The workers and the males won't survive the winter. As the air gets cold, they will die. Bumblebee might survive one more season. She and her queens will part and go underground for winter. And in spring, each bee will emerge from underground, find a suitable nest, lay her eggs, and begin once more the cycle of a bumblebee colony near the cottage on Apple Tree Lane.

About the Bumblebee

Bumblebees are found throughout the world except in arctic regions. There are at least 300 different species of bumblebees. This story was based on the species *Bombus pennsylvanicus*.

The time frame used in this story is based on the climate of southern New England. Life cycles of colonies vary from species to species and from climate to climate. For example, in warm weather climates, a colony may grow throughout the year, while a colony in a cold weather climate will only last for the warm spring and summer months.

Bumblebees can lay six to ten eggs at one time. When the young, pale-colored bees emerge from their eggs, they have matted fur and soft wings. In a very short time their bodies harden and their pale coats become vibrant shades of various colors such as yellow and black, orange and white—even shades of red.

Most wildflowers and cultivated crops could not exist in this world without the very important visits from bumblebees and other pollinators. Certain flowers have very tightly packed pollen and bumblebees have a unique way of extracting it. They vibrate their flight muscles to make a loud buzzing sound as they curl their bodies around the flower. The bee's noise vibrates the flower and the pollen is shaken out. This is called "buzz pollination." Honeybees are not able to use this extraordinary method of extracting pollen.

Glossary

cocoon: A protective covering made of silk by larvae for pupae development.

hibernation: The state of rest a bumblebee is in when she is underground for the winter.

larva: A grub-like baby bee that hatches from an egg and will develop into a pupa, then a winged adult.

nectar: A sweet, juice-like liquid that comes from plants and flowers.

pollen: A dust-like, or sometimes sticky, grainy substance, that is made by flowers.

Points of Interest in this Book

pp. 6-7: violets (purple flowers); bleeding hearts (white flowers hanging from fence).

pp. 8-9: giant crocus.

pp. 18-19: columbine (blue flowers); spotted pelidnota (beetle).

pp. 26-27: carpenter ant.

pp. 28-29: stonecrop (pink flowers).

J   PICT   48403

Gal   Galvin, Laura Gates.
             Bumblebee at Apple Tree Lane